Lisa Lynn Biggar

abuddhapress@yahoo.com

ISBN: 9798388930941

Lisa Lynn Biggar 2023

®™©

Alien Buddha Press 2023

This book is dedicated to my grandmother:

Florence Mamie Miller Jervis

TABLE OF CONTENTS

Singing	10
Unpasteurized	11
Bantee Roosters	16
Gone Visiting	21
Withers	24
Bottle Cap Fairy	27
Square Dances	31
Hurricane Agnes	34
Rabbits	37
Fassets	39
Gail	42
Potato Pancakes	44
Blackberries	48

Markus Jr.	**52**
Canoe Trips	**56**
Roslynn	**59**
Suzette	**62**
Skinny Dipping	**66**
Slow! Farm Animals	**69**
Bailing Hay	**71**
The Fort	**73**
Uncle Ross	**76**
Darren	**79**
Drive-In	**83**
Breathe	**86**
Eat	**90**

The following is a work of fiction. Any similarities to actual people, places, or events, unless deliberately expressed otherwise by the author, are purely coincidental.

SINGING

My first memory of my grandmother is standing between her legs while she drove the big blue tractor in the hay field at the top of a huge hill, the baler birthing bales of hay behind us onto the wagon where one of my uncles would stack them like a house that would never topple over, the air swarming with gnats, the sun beating down, but I have never felt happier, more content, tucked between the legs of my grandmother, singing my heart out above the din of the engine to no one.

UNPASTEURIZED

The black and white cows are locked in their stanchions, so I have a guaranteed audience, their large brown eyes following me as I dance and sing along to the country songs that blast from the speakers in the barn, while Nani scoops them their share of feed from the metal push cart, calling all thirty by their names that she painted on the wooden stanchions in white.

Sometimes I dust off my grandparents' albums in the farmhouse and play them on the old turntable: Johnny Cash, Loretta Lynn, Tammy Wynette, George Jones. . . Nani says Tammy and George had a volatile relationship— she said George liked to get drunk and knock Tammy around. Papa liked to get drunk. But he doesn't drink anymore. And I don't think he ever knocked Nani around. I can't imagine she'd let him do that. She'd hit him over the head with a frying pan before she'd let him do that. Plus, Papa has a kind heart. He never forgets to set out a warm bowl of milk for the barn cats when he's milking.

When we finish feeding the cows, we go into the milk house. Nani has to sterilize everything with strong smelling bleach. It burns my nose and stings my eyes. But since the milk is unpasteurized in the bulk tank everything has to be squeaky clean. She washes the metal milking buckets in the big stainless steel sink, and they clang like church bells while she tells me things like *what doesn't kill you makes you stronger.*

It's the end of the summer, nearly the end of our stay on the farm. My mom finished her summer course, and I have to start third grade. It's like I'm two different people—the one I am here on my grandparents' farm in northeast Pennsylvania, and the one I am in Maryland, living in a housing development surrounded by boys that try to bully me. But I'm feisty, like Nani. I give it back. Once I had Scott Cannon crying like a baby at the bus stop. I had him on the ground and wouldn't let go of his hair after he tried to choke me. That'll teach him for growing his hair long. But it is nice hair. Shiny and blond down to his shoulders.

Nani dunks the aluminum milk can in the bulk tank, fills it with unpasteurized milk. She says it's all she ever drinks. But that's not true. She keeps a bottle of vodka hidden in the bathroom. I know she's been sipping it when she comes out smelling like mouth wash. It's okay, though. It helps her get through the day. And since she raised five boys—practically on her own, she says—I guess she deserves it. My dad's the third boy. The middle one. He likes to drink, but he never drinks at home. My dad's brothers drink too, except for Trent, my youngest uncle. He's fourteen—not old enough yet. He and my dad have blue eyes like Papa with his long, slender face; the other brothers have dark eyes and more rounded faces.

Papa's parents were both from Lithuania. They built the farm and all the stone fences around the sixty acres with the stones they cleared from the hills to grow corn, hay, and oats. Nani had to live with them after she got married, and they hardly spoke any English. She never knew if they were talking about her in Lithuanian, and Nani says her mother-in-law was mean to her and that Papa always sided with his mom.

Me and Trent are pretty close, except for when I hate him. Like when he punched me in the stomach last week, knocked the wind out of me because I punched him in the head as hard as I could. For good reason, though. He was holding my dog captive between his legs, just teasing me, being mean. I ran up the hill behind the house and hid under a bush until I saw my mother's car pulling in the driveway. I could hear Nani telling her what happened, the wind carrying their voices up the hill along with the smell of potato pancakes frying. I was starving, so I came back down. Me and Trent didn't say a word to each other over supper. But we're speaking to each other again now. Nani says most things are forgivable, but I think there's a lot she's never forgiven Papa for.

BANTEE ROOSTERS

Two bantee roosters are going at it again in the front yard under the weeping willow tree. Nani has to run out with a broom to separate them. She says they'll fight to the death, and I wonder what could make them so angry—angry enough to kill or be killed.

    I watch from the kitchen window, bright feathers flying, their chests puffed out, making themselves look as big as possible. Sometimes I wonder if it isn't just a show for the chickens. But Nani says it's personal. She yells at them to "Get! Get!" shoving the broom between them. They circle each other like boxers, then scatter, maybe forgetting what it was they were even fighting about. But they say roosters are really smart. Smarter than cats and dogs—and even a four-year-old human. I'm eight, so I guess I'm smarter than those roosters. But I wonder what they think about, if they hold grudges.

Nani comes back inside. Her short hair freshly dyed marigold blonde from a box of L'Oreal. She doesn't have time or the money to go to a beauty parlor, so she does it herself. Pats her head proudly when she's finished. I don't think my grandfather ever notices, but it makes her feel pretty. Sometimes she gets all dolled up to go shopping in Wilkes-Barre, but mostly she wears loose cotton pants that come to her ankles and a sleeveless button-down cotton shirt. Unless she's in the barn, she never wears shoes. Not even in the winter. If she gets her feet dirty outside she washes them off in the toilet. I know it sounds funny, but I do it too.

  She's frying sunnies that Papa caught in the pond last night. He loves fish for breakfast. But I stick to pancakes and sausage. Sometimes eggs that I gather from the hen house. I go in there with a pail and slip my hand under the roosting hens. It's warm under there, and the eggs are warm, incubating. I don't take them all, so some little chicks can hatch.

Papa cuts the head off a chicken with a hatchet when we need one for supper. He has a bloody block of wood in the back yard for this purpose. I try not to think about it when I'm eating the fried chicken with my grandmother's mashed potatoes and gravy. Once I walked in the bathroom and there was a head of a pig in the tub. I never screamed so loud in my life. My grandmother made head cheese later that day, but I didn't want any part of that.

"What do you think they were fighting about?" I ask her now.

"Probably a chicken," she says. "Boys will be boys."

"Did you ever have boys fight over you?" I'm sitting at the kitchen table on the opposite side of where

Papa always sits. Nani never sits at the kitchen table. She has her chair by the coal stove where she sits and eats after everyone else has been fed.

"There were other boys who liked me," she says, flipping the sunnies, the grease sizzling and popping.

"But you picked Papa?"

"Your grandfather made good on a promise."

I hear him on the stairs now. He sleeps in one of the bedrooms upstairs, and Nani sleeps downstairs in the back room. She says it's on account of his snoring, but I think it's more. And I also think it's funny that she calls him Dad, like he's the father of her children but no longer her husband with a real name. He's eight years older than her, so maybe that's a reason why. I've only ever seen them kissing once—on one of the back beds upstairs. Nani jumped up when she saw me like someone lit a firecracker underneath her.

I've never seen Papa wearing anything other than overalls. And he's wearing them now, pulling the straps over his shoulders, over a white tee-shirt.

"Morning, Papa!"

"Morning, Jessie. Morning, Grace."

"It's practically noon. The cows are restless," Nani says, as she puts the sunnies on his plate with the spatula, adds some fried potatoes. Papa milks the cows at all hours of the day, but at least they get milked twice a day—that's the main thing. He asks me if I know how to spell Chicago.

"Sure," I tell him. Spell it for him.

"That's right," he says. "Chicken in the car, the car can't go. That's how you spell Chicago."

I laugh, but Nani doesn't. She's wiping her hands on her apron, looking out the kitchen window, over the endless mountains, probably thinking about Papa's promise.

GONE VISITING

Papa would call the cows back to the barn from the fields in the early evening, yelling, "Come boss! Come boss!" and I would do the same, wondering why we were calling the cows boss when they were the ones locked in the stanchions at night. Most of them would meander along willingly in a long line, but then there were the troublemakers who wanted to stay out longer, or even all night—the ones that refused to get up or would bust through the fence that constantly needed repairing. There were many days when Papa and Trent would have to go "fix fence," a big spool of barbed wire around each of their arms.

  Now and then my grandparents would get a call from one of the neighboring farms—a few of their black and white cows had gone visiting. The neighboring farms had black and white cows too, so sometimes it would take a while for them to be found out, like party crashers that fit right in. Once, when I was around nine, I went with Papa to round up a few escapees. The farmer's wife, a pretty lady with curly red hair in a yellow gingham dress sat us down and gave us each a piece of cherry pie and a glass of milk. Nani said she was from the city, that she wasn't cut out for farming. She kept winking at Papa and putting her hands on her hips, as if she were daring him to do something.

Papa never went anywhere without his fiddle. He asked her if she wanted to hear a few tunes, and when she said yes I knew it would be a long visit. He played all the usuals, "Wabash Cannonball," "Little Brown Jug," "Red Wing". . . while the lady clapped along and kicked up her heels in the kitchen. She said she felt trapped in the country, caged up.

"Everything's just so rigid 'round here," she said.

Her husband was in the barn doing the milking. He had a regular milking schedule, unlike Papa who milked his way around the clock. Nani said Papa was real good to her the two years they went together, but after they got married, on account of her getting pregnant, she said he carried on like he wasn't married, went out drinking with his friends, did things like he was still single. Papa just kept on playing, his blue eyes sparkling.

WITHERS

I read the note on the kitchen table that's in Nani's perfect cursive writing that she's so proud of, that she won an award for at her high school graduation: *Fanny cast her withers.* I say it out loud, "withers," one of the words that I only hear on the farm, like *gout, dysentery, rheumatism.* I've heard Nani say it many times, this cow or that cow cast its withers; call Lopotoski, the big animal vet.

Once he wasn't able to come, and me and Nani had to walk down the field behind the barn where the cow and its withers and calf were all in a ditch, covered in manure. I had to run back to the barn, fill a pail with soapy water. We washed off the gray-pink, slithery withers, shoved them back inside the cow; Nani told me they'd know where to go, where they belonged.

We washed off the calf, dried it with burlap bags, stood back while it found its wobbly legs. A miracle, Nani always says—especially after the ones that come out feet first, the ones that have to be pulled out with a chain and nearly choked to death before they get air. They want to stay with their mothers, but they're put in a wooden pen in the barn. I hear the mothers crying for them at night, wailing. I ask Nani why they can't be together, but she says that's just the way it has to be, that farming is hard. I close my eyes and try to close my ears, but I can't, and when I visit the calf in the morning in its small wooden pen, it sticks its nose through the rails of the pen and licks my hand, the pink tongue rough like sandpaper, tickling me, and I tell the calf that it's okay, that everything will be okay, even though I know that if it's a boy it will soon be loaded into a trailer to be sold at auction. That's just the way it has to be, Nani says, but sometimes I hear her crying at night.

BOTTLE CAP FAIRY

Normally in the summer it cooled off at night, but when there was a heat spell, me and Nani and Trent would sleep in the garage. It was a big, two car building at the end of the driveway, right next to the farm house. We kicked the cars out and put in three twin beds, a big braided rug, a flowered couch, and an old console TV set. Sometimes Trent and his friends would hang out in there, but at night it was just the three of us, the fans in the windows turned inside out to pull cool air in.

One night Trent said I should put the cap from my soda bottle under my pillow for the bottle cap fairy. I still believed in the tooth fairy then, but still, I was surprised and delighted when, the next morning, I found a dollar and a perfumed note in pink ink under my pillow from the bottle cap fairy. She said in the note that I should keep her existence a secret, as bottle caps were easier to come by than teeth. She'd never be able to keep up with the demand if everyone knew. That's how she and the tooth fairy were different. She was a secret. I asked Trent how he knew about her, and he said he just thought he'd try it one night when he was a kid (she only came to kids).

I started leaving her notes with the bottle caps—her rule was only one cap a night. I'd ask her questions like, *Do you have a body? Are you invisible? Will you ever die?* Death was something I didn't understand. When Nani's big white dog Pal was hit by a car and killed right in front of the farmhouse I kept crying and asking her, "Why? Why would God let something so terrible happen? Why does he let things die?" Nani said that Pal was in heaven with God. I went outside and yelled up at the sky at the top of my lungs, told God to throw Pal back down. But he didn't listen, so that's when I stopped talking to him, preferring to talk to the animals instead—like Dr. Dolittle—and Nani, who said she could see the eyes of God in every animal, that they knew things we didn't.

The bottle cap fairy said that only people who believed in her could see her, but she would only come when you were sleeping, so nobody really ever saw her. That was the same for the tooth fairy too, and Santa and the Easter Bunny. If you didn't fall asleep they would never come. I wondered what else went on in the world while I was sleeping.

The bottle cap fairy said that she would never die. But Trent and Nani couldn't keep the ruse going all summer—they were running out of money. They'd made the mistake of starting out with a dollar, so that was the going BCF rate. I remember feeling let down and sad but probably not too surprised. I mean, a tooth is one thing, but a bottle cap? She was real to me, though. I can still see her in that long white dress with bottle cap sequins, a crown of bottle caps on her head. For a while, her secret was safe with me.

SQUARE DANCES

Nani told me a funny story once. She said she and Papa were at a square dance—you know, where you have to have a boy as your partner. Our gym teacher has the girls make a big circle in the gym, facing the center, and then the boys have to stand behind one of us. It's so embarrassing when we have to turn around and see who picked us. Doug Clayton always picks me. And that's okay because he's kind of cute with a cowlick in his brown hair.

Anyway, Papa was playing the fiddle at the square dance and doing the calling. I don't know who Nani was dancing with. She says she was a real good dancer, so there were probably other guys more than happy to fill in for Papa—and maybe some nights when he stayed out late at the beer garden too.

On that night, though, they were both at the square dance and a storm was brewing. Nani was worried because she had left the clothes on the clothesline. One of her six sisters, Irene, and her husband Bill lived just up the road from the farm in the blue house. They were at the dance, too, and Bill was getting ready to leave early, so Nani yelled across the dance hall, "Bill, when you get home could you take my clothes off?"

Nani says she'll never live that down, but she laughs about it now, though sometimes a sadness comes over her when she talks about the dances. She went with Papa for two years before they got married, and he would take her to dances every Saturday night, but there was another guy, a fella who played the accordion, a friend of Papa's, who wanted to take her to his gigs in Lake Winola, but her mother wouldn't let her go. "No," she said, "you're going with Stan."

When they were going together, Nani says Papa would always ask her if she loved him. And she'd say, "No, but I like you a lot."

HURRICANE AGNES

I was eight when Hurricane Agnes hit the east coast in 1972. The wind and rain started when I was still in school in Maryland, early June, but after school let out and I went to my grandparents' farm for the summer, it was still raging. I don't remember the damaging winds—they were more coastal—but I do remember the many days of heavy rain. Everyone talked about building an arc, jokingly, but then seriously when the creeks and rivers started to overflow, reservoirs busting, flooding the towns, emptying out stores into the waters. People were on cliffs and bridges net fishing, bringing up bottles of alcohol, cans of food, furniture, dead animals. . . I remember a baby girl was swept away by fast-moving waters from the arms of her father.

When the rain finally subsided in early July and the waters began to recede, Trent and my older cousins decided it would be a great idea to take the inner tubes for the hay wagon tires and go tubing at the creek (we pronounced it "crick"). We'd gone tubing there before—the waterfalls gentle, forgiving—but never after a hurricane. Of course, we didn't say anything to our parents; they didn't seem to be around much. It was Nani who fed us, looked out for us on the farm; but sometimes, when it all became too much, she'd take to her bed in the backroom downstairs.

Trent, who was only fourteen then, drove the truck, with the rest of us in the open bed with the inner tubes. He liked to drive fast and crazy, swerving all over the back roads, so that we tossed and tumbled against each other like bumper cars, the inner tubes providing the only means of protection. It felt reckless, dangerous, but I refused to be left out.

We parked upstream from the swimming hole, along Route 6, piled out of the truck, grabbing our tubes. We held on to roots and branches to steady ourselves on the way down the steep dirt path of the embankment, our blood rushing through our bodies like the water over the rocks, frothing and moving fast, but this far upstream it still wasn't over our heads. We made our way out into the middle over the slippery rocks, fell in our tubes and, with whoops like cowboys, went flying—all we knew then was the rush of the water, the spray on our bodies, the roar. Our tubes spinning and plunging into the white of the falls. I don't know how close I came to drowning, but I do know that I went under and popped back up without my tube. I made it over to Trent's tube; he lifted me up onto his, the two of us spinning in our own orbit until the creek leveled out, widened, and we were able to get off to the side onto the embankment. All of us surviving and not knowing how.

RABBITS

One summer, when I was around ten, I decided to raise rabbits on the farm. I started with two white ones with black smudges on their noses. I put them in the old hen house in the backyard, covering the floor with straw. They wouldn't let me near them, but I still loved them and gave them the best care I could, buying bags of rabbit pellets at the feed store, making sure they had fresh water, and every morning I would pick them a bucket full of fresh clover. Sometimes my sister, who is six years younger than me, would help, but she would get too much grass in the bucket. I wanted them to have pure clover.

It was amazing how quickly they multiplied. Talk about a lesson in procreation. They were getting so crowded in the old hen house that I felt sorry for them, so, when the dog was inside, I'd let them out on the lawn. They didn't hop very far. I think they knew they weren't wild rabbits. Plus, who else would pick all that clover for them every morning? It was impossible to tell them apart—they were all snow white with that black smudge on their nose. One big happy family that I felt the burden of—and the end of summer was fast approaching.

My parents told me I couldn't bring them home to Maryland. And I couldn't expect Nani to take care of all of them. But I just thought she would. She cared for all of us and all the animals we no longer wanted. When we came back for Thanksgiving the first thing I did was run out back to visit my rabbits, but the old hen house was empty. And then they told me Papa had butchered all of my rabbits. They were all in the freezer at the meat locker.

I still think about those rabbits. How I deserted them.

FASSETS

Nani would drop us off at Fassets, the main department store in Tunkhannock, by the light on Main Street, while she went to the liquor store for her bottle of vodka. We'd head straight upstairs to the toy department, which comprised the whole floor—only about 800 square feet—but in our minds it was huge, a vast wonderland of treasures. We could buy anything we wanted in the cheap aisle: Super Balls, Gumby, Mr. Potato Head, jacks, marbles, dominoes, the very toxic Super Elastic Bubble Plastic... Once I bought a kaleidoscope. It was made out of cardboard, but I thought it was the most magical thing in the world. I spent hours looking through it, beautiful, colorful patterns emerging, coming into focus.

When Nani was around ten her mother would put her on the milk truck, barefoot in a hand-sewn dress, with a crate of eggs to trade for groceries in Tunkhannock. Nani would worry that the eggs wouldn't be enough for the groceries, but every time it came out even. Afterwards, she'd wait on the corner where a ten- cent store used to be, where Fassets now was. She said it was frightening, but Mr. Palmer, the milkman, never forgot to return for her.

    The main floor of Fassets had clothes, hats, shoes, cards, gifts, cameras. . . Once Nani bought Trent a big, fat instamatic camera there for his birthday, the pictures miraculously popping out of the front of the camera. You had to wait a few minutes before peeling off the self-developing film, pulling the positive from the negative—the black and white images miraculously developing before our eyes.

    Sometimes Nani would pull out the box of yellowed black and white pictures of relatives—their names scrawled in cursive on the back with the date. She'd point out our distant relatives, people we had never known. And she'd tell us about her hard-working Polish mother, one leg crippled from polio, who raised nine children on the dairy farm up the road, half the time on her own because Nani's stern German father couldn't take the cold. He went to live with his parents in Harrisburg every winter, where Nani said he was probably drinking and chasing women because he never sent any money home.

At Christmas, though, her father would come back around and dress up like Santa. Her mother would hold a kerosene lantern at the bottom of the stairs and yell, "Wake up! Wake up! I think I hear Santa coming!" And then her father would ring a bell and climb the stairs with a big bag on his back. He'd ask Nani if she'd been a good girl, and when she nodded shyly, he'd reach into his bag and pull out a doll and put it in her arms. "Oh, what a thrill that was!" she'd say with a smile.

GAIL

The fire spread like lightning through the barn up the road where twenty-four heifers were housed, a lantern falling on the bales of hay in the loft. Nani could hear the terrified cries of the cows, but there was nothing she could do, nothing anyone could do, the fire department arriving too late. They were only babies, Nani cried over and over on the phone. They never had a chance. And now I wonder if this made her think of her second baby, a baby girl, a seemingly healthy baby who died of crib death at only ten hours old. A girl she'd named Gail, followed by four more boys.

    Nani mourned all summer for those heifers. I was eleven then, and I didn't understand why she kept reliving this nightmare over and over. I hated to see her cry, but I didn't know what to do to comfort her, and she was spending more time in the bathroom during the day, coming out smelling like Listerine, sometimes passing out late afternoon on the bed in the back room downstairs. Once, when she was in that state, she called me to her bedside, said she was afraid of getting old, of dying, and I held her, but I wanted to run away. She was supposed to be the strong one. I didn't want to have to hold her up. But she called me Gail, told me I was her lost baby, her calloused hands on my face, hugging me to her chest.

POTATO PANCAKES

The trick is getting them crispy on the outside, without being too greasy, and chewy on the inside. We always knew when Nani was going to make them because she'd bring up pounds of potatoes from the root cellar. The preparations would start mid-morning. She'd peel the potatoes and put them in cold water, then grate them in a bowl, using the smallest holes on the grater, then grate onions into the same bowl.

"You have to pour off the liquid now," she'd say. "You don't want soggy pancakes—they'll never fry up."

Then you beat eggs in another bowl, add them to the potatoes, add flour, salt, and pepper and mix well. She had a Teflon-coated aluminum pan she used to fry them in, pouring just the right amount of peanut oil in first, about a quarter-inch deep.

"Can't drown them," she'd say, spreading out the batter for each pancake with a spoon in the pan. "Turn them when the edges are brown, and only turn them once."

She'd serve them with sour cream, apple sauce, and ketchup, but we made fun of anyone who put ketchup on them. Ketchup was for her homemade French fries, which she made less frequently and served with hamburgers. She'd place a platter in the middle of the table with a paper towel on it to absorb the grease, then place the pancakes on it with her spatula, all of us sitting around the kitchen table, grabbing greedily.

None of us could make potato pancakes as good as her, try as we may. We had different theories: it was the skillet she used, the homegrown potatoes, the blood, sweat, and tears that went into making so many. The onions would make her cry, but now I wonder. . . When she started frying up that first batch, without fail, people would start pulling up the driveway, like the force of gravity on water: neighbors, friends, other relatives. . . People would just stop by then. Go visiting. But somehow they always knew when it was potato pancake day. My grandmother never complained, though. She'd just go down in the cellar for another pound of potatoes and keep peeling and grating and frying until we could barely move, boasting about the number of pancakes we'd eaten. It wasn't until we were all finished that she'd fix herself a plate, sitting down on her chair by the coal stove that had "happy thoughts" engraved on the front.

  I wonder what she was thinking then, if she was content in having fed so many, or if it crossed her mind to just run away, become that nurse she said she always wanted to be. Or if she was thinking about Albert, the boy she used to help with his studies in high school, the boy she talked her teacher into not flunking, who had been in love with her but was too shy to ask her out.

There were six other students in her graduating class. At the graduation ceremony they all dressed like sailors in navy and white and sang songs about sailing away to distant lands.

BLACKBERRIES

Uncle Vince, the next to youngest of my father's four brothers, had five children with his wife, Patty. Mary was the oldest, one year younger than me. Vince and Patty built a house just down the road from my grandparents' farm, so it was easy for Mary and me to get together in the summer, but it wasn't that often. Vince and Patty didn't seem to trust outside influences on their kids, not even family—they kept their kids close to home.

So it was a rather rare occurrence that Mary and I spent any time alone together. I wasn't to be trusted and neither were my older cousins. But I remember one time I invited her to go picking blackberries with me when I was around eleven. A few things to note about my blackberry expeditions: Just like on Halloween when I refused to call it a night until my bag was filled with candy, I wouldn't call it a day until my silver milk pail was filled to the brim with berries. I'd pack a lunch for the long day's haul, drinking ice cold water from an underground spring with cupped hands, the sun close to setting before I'd trudge home, then fill a bowl with berries and milk and sugar as my reward, Nani baking pies and tarts with the rest. Sometimes I'd go with my older cousins, who were nearly as intrepid, but Mary was *never* allowed to hang out with our older cousins.

But that day it was just Mary and me. She walked up to the farm early in the morning, not at all dressed for the expedition in shorts, a tank top, and flip flops. I had to get her one of my long-sleeved cotton shirts and a pair of my jeans. We were both average height and slender, though people would call Mary thin and me fit, and even in the summer Mary looked pale, Nani often making her chicken soup when she wasn't feeling well. For shoes she had to wear a pair of Nani's barn boots which were loose on her and made her walk clumsily. But off we went with our sandwiches and milk pails, walking behind the barn, down to the stream that was teeming with little gold minnows, crossing over on a bridge of stones, then climbing the steep hill to the stone fence where most of the berry bushes were.

Mary complained the whole way about her shoes, the bugs, the heat. It was early August, the morning sun already steaming, gnats flying in our eyes, ears, nose. I have to say she gave it her best shot. She climbed the stone wall, started filling her pail, but then she pricked her finger, and it started bleeding. She started to cry.

"Stop acting like a baby!" I yelled. Nani always told me to be kind to Mary, but I was in no mood for sissies, and I already regretted asking her to come on my expedition. What had always felt freeing, a whole day away from adults, felt cumbersome now. I didn't want the responsibility of Mary. And I blamed myself, knowing she wasn't cut out for this. But I thought I could change her, make her tougher.

And then she saw a spider, a harmless garden spider, but they're big and yellow and black with scary-looking zigzag shapes on their webs. She screamed, falling off the wall, spilling her meager show of berries. She was okay, but she was done for the day. She walked back down the hill, crying. And I didn't go after her. I was determined to fill my whole pail. And that I did, singing my heart out into the waning light, my hands stained with berry juice, like blood.

MARKUS JR.

Markus Jr. came to live on the farm for a while when he was thirteen, when his mom couldn't handle him anymore. I think Nani wanted to try and save him like she couldn't save her cousin, who died at age fifteen after a night of drinking and deviling with his friends. Markus Jr. was only a few years older than me, my Uncle Markus's youngest son of three. My uncle was living on the farm then too, between divorces; he drove truck for a living, so he wasn't there much, but when he was he'd get drunk at night and whip Markus Jr. with his belt in front of the milk house. When we were there in the summer, my mom and I'd watch out the window of one of the upstairs bedrooms in the farm house. Markus Jr. would yell, but that only made my uncle strike him harder. It seemed to be an unspoken rule that each of my dad's brothers did what they wanted to with their kids—no one dared interfere, not even Nani.

Once my parents invited Markus Jr. to go on a daytrip to the Poconos with us. The two of us in the backseat. I thought he was cute with his tousled blonde hair that fell over his blue eyes and his mischievous grin. I remember I had on red shorts and a blue and white striped tube top. It was a hot summer day, and my dad's Buick didn't have air conditioning, so we had all of the windows down, my long brown hair flying all around. Markus Jr. had on shorts too and our thighs were sticking to the back seat. We kept peeling them off the seat to cool ourselves, but when I put mine back down they splayed out more than his, and he started making fun of this, calling me chubby thighs. My parents lost in their own conversation.

At the Poconos we went to a petting zoo. I remember being surrounded by animals that wanted the dry food we bought from the dispensers. There were ponies and goats, donkeys and deer, a pot-bellied pig, chickens, ducks. . . Markus Jr. pinched the skin between my tube top and shorts and said I must be related to the pig. I kicked him and said he looked like the donkey. Then I said something I wish I'd never said. I told him he had a fat ass, that I'd seen it from the bedroom window when his father was whipping him. "And bet you deserved it!" I yelled. By then the animals were wandering away from us. They didn't want any more of what we had to give.

    Markus Jr. didn't say much on the way home, and not long after that he moved back into the trailer with his mother. I'd hear things now and then about the trouble he'd get into. About the times he ran away. The times he got caught stealing. The times he went to jail. His life wasn't going anywhere, so it wasn't much of a tragedy, I heard a few say, when a lady, a drunk driver, swerved her car off the road on a foggy night and hit him. He shouldn't have been walking on the side of the road at night in a fog. He shouldn't have been wearing black. He probably shouldn't have been born, some people even said. He was a bad seed. Guess he deserved to die at seventeen. And nothing ever happened to the lady, a friend of the judge in town, who just drove away and said later she thought she'd hit a deer.

CANOE TRIPS

I was bound and determined my dad and I would have the lightest canoe. I'd sneak around while we were all preparing to launch, replacing any of the heavy bags in our canoe with lighter ones, so when we shoved off my dad and I were sitting highest on the water. And then we'd dip our paddles into the Susquehanna, begin the rhythmic rowing, navigating around rocks in the rush of the mild rapids—I was the eyes in the front, my dad in the back steering. We were always sore after the first day, but then we dug in deeper, grew stronger.

    My Uncle Ross and his son George were in another canoe. Trent and Uncle Ross's daughter Cindy in another, her long brown hair that I envied down to her butt in her yellow bikini. Mary rode in the middle of a canoe between her dad and my Uncle Markus. She didn't do any of the rowing, and I thought how boring that must've been.

At night, Mary and I would make s'mores and then slip inside our sleeping bags, the shadows from the crackling campfire dancing on the walls of the tent, my dad and his brothers passing around a bottle, singing their favorite songs: "Jean," "Those Were the Days," "Que Sera Sera". . . They all had rich voices with a natural vibrato, like mine—singing the thing that came easiest to me, but I didn't think of trying to make it as a singer then; I thought I wanted to work with animals, maybe be a veterinarian.

Once I asked Mary what she wanted to be, and she said she didn't know, but she definitely wanted to get married, have a few kids, a dog. Maybe she would be a dental hygienist. She liked teeth.

"Why not a dentist?" I asked.

She shrugged. I think she was thinking that only men could be dentists, but I didn't say anything. I understood that Mary just wanted a simple life. She didn't want to push boundaries or make a big splash in the world. She just wanted to go along for the ride—unlike Nani who had desperately wanted to go to college, become a nurse, make a life of her own—not get knocked up at seventeen, then married, the two neighboring farms eventually joined together like an inexorable fate.

ROSLYNN

Roslynn was Trent's girlfriend when he was a junior and senior in high school. She was an only child whose parents didn't get along. One summer when Trent went to band camp for a week, I hung out with Roslynn, kept her company. She didn't seem to have any other friends. We went roller-skating and swimming in ponds, and when I spent the night at her house we ate dinner with her parents, who never spoke a word to each other, like Nani's father who had bouts with depression and would go for months without speaking a word to anyone. Nani said he'd come to the table and put his head down and then go out back and sit on the stoop and smoke his pipe.

Roslynn wanted to be a model. She had a nice body, curvy with big boobs, but she had acne pretty bad on her face. She went to a dermatologist and took big white pills, but it didn't seem to do any good. I felt sorry for her. I wished I could cut away those blemishes, make her pretty. Her eyes were blue, a little crossed; sometimes she looked a little crazy, like she wasn't all there.

 I remember listening to records in her room. 45s. "Love Will Keep Us Together" was the big hit that summer. Everyone had that record by Captain and Tennille, and every time you turned on the radio, there it was. Roslynn thought she and Trent were going to get married, that they would be together forever. I wasn't so sure. I could see Trent backing away at times, hiding from her, not answering the phone. He would tell Nani to answer, have her tell Roslynn that he was in town or in the shower. There were no cell phones back then. So sometimes Roslynn would just drive around, looking for him.

 Once I went to Scranton with her to buy a shiny, new gold Camaro. Her father owned some kind of lumber business, so Roslynn pretty much got whatever she wanted. She had all kinds of clothes and shoes, and that day she wanted a brand new car. So we bought the one right off the showroom floor of the car dealer, drove it to the farm to show it off that day.

My cousins were crazy about it, and Cindy asked to drive it. She drove it fast down the road past the farm, too fast to make the turn that hooked right and drove the brand new car straight into a swamp. Trent had to pull it out with a tractor, and it was no longer gold, rather a murky green. The inside of the car was ruined. Cindy was devastated. But Roslynn just drove it back to the car dealer and returned it for a shimmering, silver Camaro. Her daddy paid for both of those cars. Like I said, Roslynn pretty much got whatever she wanted. Except for Trent.

SUZETTE

My dad or one of my uncles would go get the clams in the morning, around four bushels, and then put them in the tub of the downstairs bathroom so we could scrub them. My cousins and I would work in shifts, scrubbing the sand off them (the worst was eating a clam that wasn't scrubbed properly, the grit crunching between your teeth). My dad would be in charge of steaming the clams on the stove on the back porch. Platter after platter of clams, served with melted butter, would be placed on the tables in the backyard of the farmhouse.

    Nearly all the family would be at the yearly clam bakes, extended family as well, along with friends and neighbors. Uncle Vince would grill the chicken, Nani would cook the corn on the cob, straight off the stalk into the pot. My mother would make the baked beans, Aunt

Patty the decadent Texas Sheet Cake. Others would bring potato salad, macaroni salad, coleslaw, deviled eggs, ambrosia salad with Cool Whip...

When we were finally full, Trent and my cousins and I would spray paint the clam shells and sell them as ash trays for twenty-five cents each. Most of the adults smoked back then and drank lots of beer. Once I spray painted a clam shell black and then painted "smoking kills" on it with white paint. Uncle Markus bought it, laughing. But it wasn't a joke. Smoking killed my best friend's mom who was dating Uncle Ross then—my dad's oldest brother who'd been divorced a while. I can still see her smoking a cigarette like a movie star at one of the clam bakes, her long, teased red hair, dyed blonde, her long legs and arms freckled. Suzette had a throaty voice that hinted at what was to come—but back then she was more alive than anyone I'd ever known.

She and my Uncle Ross were crazy together. Once I saw them coming out of the cornfield at night buck naked under the light of a full moon. They looked bewildered, as if they'd just been thrown down on this earth from Eden, blinking in the bright of the light.

That day, at the clam bake, Suzette was sitting on my uncle's lap, talking about dreams, the meaning of them. She had checked out every book about dreams at her local library. That's what she would do—completely immerse herself in one subject at a time.

"A snake means someone's imminent death," she said, blowing out smoke.

"I can fly in my dreams," my uncle said. "I soar all over the world."

"That's your soul flying," she said. "We forget that we can fly."

I asked her if she wanted to buy a clam shell.

"Sure," she said, picking out a bright pink one for her ashes.

SKINNY DIPPING

The summer after my dad and his brothers gave up on the week-long canoe trips down the Susquehanna, he and Uncle Vince took my cousin, Mary, and me camping—just down the road from the farm. I was around twelve then, Mary eleven. We set up tents on an embankment above the Tunkhannock Creek. It was only for a night, but Aunt Patty still resented it and brought my uncle a big bucket of yellow beans to cut the ends off for canning.

    Uncle Vince was fuming, so Mary and I slipped away and found a winding path down to the creek. We weren't planning on swimming, didn't even have our bathing suits. But when we dipped our toes in, the coolness was irresistible, the gentle current lapping over the rocks along the shore. We called up to our dads, the campfire illuminating their faces, the green bottles of beer, a cigarette dangling from my uncle's lips as he chopped the ends off the beans. I don't remember if my dad helped him, but I'm sure he did after teasing him for a while. He's softhearted like that. We asked them if we could go in.

"Sure," they yelled back. "Just be careful."

Mary wanted to swim with our clothes on, but I convinced her to go skinny dipping. "No one can see us," I said. "It's pitch dark." The stars were bright, twinkling eyes, too far away to spy. The moon just a wink in the sky.

She hesitantly agreed and we shed our clothes, giggling, then eased our way in over the slippery rocks. The water cooling, caressing our bodies, carrying us away; we had to doggie paddle against the current, against time.

Minnows tickled our feet, but it was the larger fish, the carp, that frightened us—the fish that nobody wanted to catch because they're tough and loaded with bones. One of them jumped out of the water beside us and Mary screamed. Our fathers called down to ask what was wrong, and I said nothing, that it was only a fish.

    I told Mary they wouldn't hurt us, but I remember that moment—the carp circling us, so vulnerable in our nakedness. And the feeling that our fathers could no longer protect us from the vastness of the universe. The campfire slowly burning itself out.

SLOW! FARM ANIMALS

My parents didn't really get the dog thing. Or maybe it was the dogs. At any rate, all the dogs we had when I was young ended up on the farm—Nani taking in as many unwanted dogs as she did troubled kids. Benji, a hound mix, the last dog we left on the farm, had just been killed on the back road in front of the farm house. I was so tired of people speeding on that road, killing numerous animals. I decided to make two big signs to put alongside the road on both ends of the farm. Glen, my sort-of boyfriend, volunteered to help me. He was around fifteen then, three years older than me. We found some plywood in the shed behind the house, and I painted *Slow Farm Animals* on them. Glen cracked up over that—he said it sounded like the animals on the farm were all demented, so that's when I learned the power of punctuation: I added an exclamation mark. Glen nailed the signs to wooden posts, and then he sledge-hammered them into the side of the road. They stayed up for about a week before the road crew took them down, said they got in the way of mowing. I was mad about that, but for a week the cars did slow down, and even after the signs were gone they kept slowing down. That's when I learned the power of words, too—how they stay with you, how they linger. . . It was around that time that Glen told me he loved me. I was so young, I didn't know what to do with those words, but I kept them in my heart, on reserve.

BAILING HAY

Trent would drive the tractor, and Glen and I would be on the wagon where the baler would pop out the bales of hay. I would grab them by the twine that bound them and throw them back to Glen who would stack them in a way the structure wouldn't topple over when we made our way back down the hill on the bumpy dirt road.

Glen and I would sit on top of the bales on the way down, holding hands, as if we were a married couple, proud of the construction of our new home, only to tear it down when we got back to the barn, sending each bale up the elevator shaft to the hay loft. It was just me on the wagon then, placing the bales on the elevator, sending them up to Glen in the loft, the elevator like the electricity between us. He'd come back down covered in hay, soaked in sweat, and I thought he was cuter than ever then. I'd ruffle his unruly brown hair to get the hay out, and I know he wanted to kiss me, but I was young, only thirteen or fourteen, so we only kissed in the dark.

    Nani thought I was sleeping in the garage with Trent and my cousins, but Glen and I would slip away into Trent's tent set up in the back yard, sharing a sleeping bag, rolling around and kissing all night long, his tongue tasting like purple Kool-Aid, his body hard against mine. He'd be sure to be gone by morning, running home, sneaking back into his own bed, and I'd sneak back into one of the beds in the garage. I don't know if Nani suspected—if she did, she never said anything, never warned me that Glen could get me pregnant, that I'd have to raise a baby instead of go to college, but Glen never took it too far, unlike Papa, who said if he got Nani in trouble he'd marry her— and he'd kept his promise.

THE FORT

We called it the fort, although it looked more like a little house with its blue siding and windows and tar paper roof, wooden steps from the front door leading down to the forest ground—no railing, so after we'd had a few beers—Genesee Cream Ale—we'd climb up the stairs like monkeys, using our hands to help navigate, balance.

    There was rust-colored carpet inside, burnt in places from joints and cigarettes. And a few band posters on the white-washed walls—Heart, Three Dog Night, Grand Funk Railroad . . . Most nights, though, unless it rained, we'd hang out in the woods below the fort, around a small bonfire, drinking beer and shooting shit like we were all grown up, our parents none the wiser.

    I was around thirteen then, too young to hang out with my older cousins, but too old to be left out. One night Cindy and Keith were in the fort getting high with some of the neighbor kids, and I got it in my head that pot could kill you; I knew I had to save them. I climbed up the wooden steps and banged on one of the glass panes of the door so hard that my hand went through, shattering the glass, showering my naked cousins with shards of glass, leaving small cuts. But my wrist was slit, a gash in the artery, the blood spilling like a fountain.

    Glen made me a tourniquet out of his shirt, crying, afraid for my life. I should've gone to the hospital, but we were all too drunk, too scared. Glen kept telling me that he loved me, that I couldn't die, and I felt a sense of power, never believing that I would die, but knowing that if I did, Glen would never be the same, that he would never get over me, like Nani never got over Albert, who jumped out a window when he found out she was getting married.

    Eventually, my wrist stopped bleeding, but Roslynn, who seemed older than any of us with her big boobs and bleached blond hair, kept spinning around in the field outside the woods in the moonlight, screaming like a wild banshee, as if she'd lost her mind.

UNCLE ROSS

Uncle Ross, my dad's oldest brother, would knock his first martini back in practically one gulp, then sip his martinis the rest of the day on the farm, reminiscing about all the good times he and his brothers had growing up there. Most nights he'd just pass out, but other times he became reckless, unpredictable. Once he grew angry and decided that he and my cousins, George and Cindy, were going back to Wisconsin in the middle of the night—a thirteen-hour drive from my grandparents' farm. Even Nani couldn't stop him.

One summer night I was making out with Glen in the back of my grandparent's station wagon. We never went too far, not even heavy petting, but he was giving me a pretty good hickey when my uncle's round, red face appeared at the window, a mass of dark curls framing his irate features: bloodshot eyes, flared nostrils, profanities slurring from his mouth—the things he was going to do to Glen, who couldn't get out of the car fast enough. Glen went flying through the cornfield, my uncle chasing after him, but I wasn't worried—I knew my uncle wasn't in any shape to navigate the maze.

I stayed in the car for a while, expecting Uncle Ross to come back, but I wasn't afraid of him. I knew he'd never lay a hand on me. He adored my father, the middle brother, so much so that he'd always been jealous of me, but I knew he'd never hurt me. My dad said he had a heart of gold when he wasn't drinking. I wasn't so sure, but he did love his kids, his springer spaniel, all the trees he was always planting on his own farm in Wisconsin.

I went back into the farmhouse, Papa finishing up the milking in the barn—he was a night owl, so the cows had to be too—my cousins and Trent probably still at the fort, drinking beer with some neighbor kids. Nani, up before the sun, long gone to bed. I grabbed a cinnamon-apple pop tart, went upstairs to the bedroom where I slept. There was an adjoining bathroom with a window that looked out over the side of the house, the moon like a laser beam over the cornfield. I ate my pop tart and listened to the riot of the bugs, watched for Glen to come out from the corn, but I knew he'd run all the way back home, thinking a madman was on his heels.

DARREN

My cousin Darren and I were parked in front of the side doors of the round-roof barn my grandparents had built to replace the one that burned down. It was a more modern barn that kept the snow off the roof, but it didn't have the charm of the old barn with its hay loft—a perfect place to read or nap when it wasn't stifling hot, not to mention what Trent and Roslynn did in there.

    We were in Darren's gold Gran Torino, drinking bottles of Rolling Rock, talking about the fire. He was Uncle Markus's oldest son, a year older than Trent, but Trent was still his uncle and that pissed him off. Sometimes he and Trent would get into fist fights, and it seemed like they wanted to kill each other—only Nani could make them stop. She had a soft spot in her heart for Darren, her first grandchild, and that pissed Trent off.

Darren came to live on the farm when he was a senior, when his mother kicked him out of the trailer. "Grandma's never gotten over that fire," he said, tipping the beer bottle to his lips. He was around twenty-one then, had big, brown, puppy-dog eyes, a lazy smile. A way of teasing, confidant in his charms. My mother didn't trust him, but she probably had a crush on him too.

"She said she still has nightmares about it," I said, thinking how awful it must have been to hear the desperate cries of those twenty-four heifers, to feel so helpless.

"She blames herself for leaving that lantern on." His voice had a slow drawl to it as if he'd already moved to Georgia, married his second wife, had three more boys that he deserted.

"She didn't knock it over," I said, putting my legs up on the dashboard. I was aware of my own charms by then too, my slender frame, my green, cat-like eyes.

"Guess it was a ghost," he said, poking me in the side, sending a jolt through me.

"You believe in ghosts?" he asked.

I shrugged, took a sip of beer. "Yeah, I guess. Some people just wanna stick around and cause trouble."

"Or maybe they cause trouble because they're stuck here," Darren said, lighting up a cigarette. He asked me if I wanted one; I shook my head. Last time I'd tried smoking it made me sick—that and too many beers. We were quiet then, the moon beaming down, casting shadows over the rolling hills.

"I'm never gonna be stuck here," Darren said, blowing smoke out his window. "If I wanna leave, I'll leave."

I knew he was talking about his girlfriend Dawn then. She was pressuring him to marry her; I think she was pregnant. She wanted him to get a job at the Charmin plant where Uncle Vince worked. Settle down. But Darren wasn't the settling kind, like Papa—I wonder how many times he thought of packing up his fiddle, leaving the farm and his family behind.

Darren did end up marrying Dawn, though, worked at Charmin for a while, and had another son, before they divorced and he split for Georgia.

"You can do whatever you want," I said.

"Oh yeah?" he said, leaning in like he was gonna kiss me, his face close to mine, his breath warm. I wanted him to, but he never did.

Guess he knew better.

DRIVE-IN

We'd pile in the car, and then the rest of us would hide in the trunk on the way in to the drive-in movie. You only had to be in the trunk for a short time and it saved money (you paid by the car to get into the movie; I think it was $5). We'd go to the first row and spread blankets down on the grass. Glen and I would lie down beside each other holding hands, kissing when the movie started. We never really paid attention to the movies: *Van, Empire of the Ants, Children of the Corn*... That one got to me though—for weeks I'd wait for creepy little kids to come out of the cornfield on my grandparents' farm, brandishing little hatchets. Glen jumped out from behind a cornstalk once, scaring the shit out of me. I chased him until he let me catch him, tackle him to the ground, wrestle him in the grass, tickling each other to tears.

When I was sixteen, maybe seventeen, Trent and my cousins and I went to the drive-in to see *Young Frankenstein*. There weren't so many of us then, so no one had to hide in the trunk. When we got there, Trent pointed out Glen's green '69 Camaro, the one I used to drive on the back roads, sitting between Glen's legs. At first he just let me steer, but, eventually, he gave me total control—like I had over him back then.

But when I went back home to Maryland after the summers I didn't care about my hold on Glen. I had my school friends, my studies, cheerleading, other boys. For some reason, though, I thought things would always be the same between me and Glen. I thought when I got to the farm he'd always be back around, chasing me down.

We pulled up beside Glen's car at the drive-in, and he had a girl with him. A blonde girl, her jaw and nose pointed in profile. That's all I really noticed, as I had to look away, pretend I didn't care, Trent and my cousins all watching me. I don't know if Glen even knew I was in the car; Trent knew enough to find another place to park.

"We'll give you some privacy," he said to them, making me wince.

Trent and my cousins laughed their guts out over that movie and walked and talked like Igor for weeks afterwards, but I'm not sure I even cracked a smile.

BREATHE

I tried a year of college out of high school, but I kept changing my major like the color of my hair, so I decided to move to New York City to try and make it as a singer. I lived in Long Island City, Queens, in the basement of a Greek family's home, where I slept on a mattress on the floor and had a small bathroom with a shower. The Greek family didn't speak any English (I found the room through a realtor), so they left me alone, and I was only there to sleep anyway.

In the mornings, I took the subway into Manhattan, looking for my big break, taking dance and singing lessons and playing the piano once a week for an old lady who gave me fifty bucks for the half hour but always told me I needed more practice. I also waitressed, of course, and did some back-stage work for an off-off-Broadway show. I had to crouch back-stage in the dark and turn a big crank on cue to revolve the stage. I remember how the lead actor and actress would kiss passionately before going on stage. They said they did it to get the spark going between them for the performance, but I wondered (the actor was married).

Most weekends I'd take the bus back to my grandparents' dairy farm. Trent would pick me up in Scranton. He was living in the pink house then—the two-story house just up the road from my grandparents' farm, the house Nani grew up in. It wasn't pink anymore, but we still called it that. I liked to hang out there when Trent wasn't home and do yoga or one of his Chippendale exercise videos. I was there in the evening one Saturday doing yoga when someone knocked on the side door in the kitchen. It was Glen returning Trent's chain saw—lightning had recently downed a tree by his trailer. We were surprised to see each other—it had been probably over a year. I was nineteen then; he was twenty-two. He looked more grown up, manly, his lips set in a thin line, as if he'd decided to take a neutral position on life, not expecting to be happy or unhappy.

I asked him if he wanted to hang out for a while, maybe watch a movie. There was an awkward silence for a moment—I could tell he was considering it—but then he said his girlfriend was waiting in the car, that they were going to dinner. My heart sank. I felt so foolish. Glen had moved on, but here I was, alone, thinking things could be rekindled between us.

"Oh, well, have fun," I said, trying to sound casual.

"It was good to see you," Glen said, our eyes meeting, hesitating.

I think he may have kissed me if his girlfriend hadn't been there, probably looking in the kitchen window, but he turned and walked away, and I closed the door behind him, the teacher in the yoga video reminding me to breathe.

EAT

I took the late bus out of Port Authority to Scranton. My hair cut short and dyed blonde after a bout with black and then red hair. Trent and Glen picked me up. They'd had a few beers at a bar across from the station. I was surprised to see Glen with Trent—last I knew he was still with his girlfriend. I gave Trent a hug but felt awkward around Glen, the attraction still there, but things were different now. The world felt so much larger.

"I had to get out of that city," I said, climbing in the back seat of Trent's Buick, throwing my duffle bag on the seat.

"What happened?" Trent asked in his thick Pennsylvania accent—an accent I'd never noticed when I was younger.

"I stepped over a man," I said. "He rolled down the steps of a church right in front of me. And I stepped over him, kept right on walking—didn't even look back."

"Was he dead?" Glen asked.

"I don't know," I said. "I think he was drunk or on drugs. But I don't know."

The three of us were quiet for a moment. It started to rain, the windshield wipers squeaking a somber tune, the streets of Scranton dark and quiet, so unlike New York City that never sleeps. But I needed sleep now, my nerves on edge, my mind restless. I wondered if I was just wasting time trying to make it as a singer. So much competition. So much talent. Everyone hungry. But I kept my doubts to myself, said I'd seen Madonna filming a movie on the Upper West Side while I was walking to my voice lessons the other day. Trent couldn't believe it; he was a huge

Madonna fan. But Glen didn't seem impressed. I don't think he liked to think of me any place other than the farm.

He was living in a trailer just down the road from the farmhouse then. I had turned twenty-one that past winter, Glen twenty-four. He asked us if we wanted to hang out, watch a movie. Trent said he had to get up early, do the milking—my grandfather retired now. But I said, sure. I thought maybe this was it, maybe Glen and I would finally sleep together—maybe we were meant to be together after all.

Trent dropped me and Glen off in front of the plain brown and white trailer. I admired the zinnias planted around the lighted cement porch.

"Had to do something to dress it up," he said.

We went inside and Glen got us a couple bottles of beers out of the fridge—Yuengling, a step up from the

Genesee Cream Ale we used to drink at the fort. We sat down at the small round kitchen table. Glen said he was so sorry to hear about Mary, how she'd recently been diagnosed with leukemia, that the bone marrow transplant hadn't been a success. I told him I was going to the hospital tomorrow to see her, something I was dreading.

"You never know," he said, drawing out the syllables, his accent as thick as Trent's.

Glen had gone to work at Charmin, the factory where nearly everyone works who sticks around Tunkhannock now that Bendix was closed in Montrose—where Nani worked the night shift for ten years, fitting stators into armatures, making money to send my dad and Uncle Ross to Penn State. A job that got her off the farm; a job, she said, she loved.

"I hate it there," Glen said. "Same damn thing every day. I just count the minutes 'til my shift is over."

I didn't know what to say. Part of me envied that monotony, that false sense of knowing what each hour would bring.

"Well, at least you're making good money," I finally said.

"Yeah, but I'm counting the days 'til I can retire," he said, taking a gulp of beer.

I knew I didn't want to live that way, wishing my life away. There had to be a way to love your life *and* make money. I wasn't making it as a singer in NYC, but maybe if I started out smaller, maybe if I moved to the farm, started a country band. . .

"What do you wanna watch?" Glen asked.

"What do you have?"

He opened his cabinet by the TV. Most of the movies I wasn't interested in—Schwarzenegger movies, Indiana Jones, James Bond. . . I chose *Grease*. Everyone owned that movie back then, and no one ever got sick of watching it. Glen put it in the VHS player, and we started watching it on the black leather couch, sitting close together but not touching—I couldn't help but think about *our* summer loving, rolling around in the tent, and how long ago it all seemed now.

It wasn't long before Glen was fast asleep. Before he even kissed me. It was Friday—he had worked all week, and he'd drunk a lot of beer. I didn't feel rejected as much as let down. But I told myself it was for the best. I really couldn't see myself living in a trailer, waiting for my husband to come home from the factory. And, truth be told, I don't think I ever loved Glen. I just loved being loved by him for that short time.

I walked up the road to my grandparents' farmhouse. It was the end of summer, the bugs on the wane, the debate about whether Katy did it dying down without a verdict. The light was still on in the kitchen, the door unlocked. Nani's macaroni and cheese casserole on the coal stove. It was my favorite, made with her canned tomatoes, white American cheese slices browned on top. Her Steno notepad open on the kitchen table: *Be sure and eat, Jessie. I love you, Nani.*

She said it was her family that kept her going, memories of her hard-working mother. And then I thought of what she would always say to me, that no one can take your education away. I decided that I would go back to college, learn as much as I could. I would never be a nurse or a veterinarian—that wasn't in me—but I would live a life of my own.

THANK YOU

Dan Crawley, for cheering me on and finding the thread that pulled this work together

Rachel Hicks, for your fine copy editing skills

Alien Buddha Press, for giving this work a home

Don Biggar, husband extraordinaire, who lent a sharp eye to this work and makes the best breakfasts in the world

Mom and Dad, for believing in me

ACKNOWLEDGEMENTS

These stories first appeared, a few in somewhat different form, in the following journals:

- "Singing" published by *Scribes *Micro* Fiction* (March 2023)
- "Suzette" published by *Random Sample* under the title "Clambake" (March 2023)
- "Markus Jr." published by *Pithead Chapel* under the title "Alex Jr." (Aug. 2022)
- "Skinny Dipping" published by *Schuylkill Valley Journal* (July 2022)

ABOUT THE AUTHOR

Lisa Lynn Biggar received her MFA in Fiction from Vermont College. Her short fiction has appeared in numerous literary journals, including *Main Street Rag, Bluestem Magazine, The Minnesota Review, Kentucky Review, The Delmarva Review, Litro Magazine, Superstition Review* and *Pithead Chapel.* She's the fiction editor for *Little Patuxent Review* and co-owns and operates a cut flower farm on the eastern shore of Maryland with her husband and two hard working cats.

www.writinglisa.com

twitter.com/lislafleur

www.facebook.com/lisa.biggar

instragram.com/lislafleur1

Made in the USA
Columbia, SC
30 July 2023